ADHD Warrior

The Journey of a Girl with ADHD

Annamaria RZ

Editor: Athena B

"Dedicated to all individuals with ADHD, both those diagnosed and those undiagnosed, yet still navigating its consequences."

Introduction

This book is a reflection of my life and the lives of others like me. The names, time and places are all fictional. Even though some parts are based on real life experiences, it is still mostly fictional. As you turn these pages, you'll encounter moments of doubt, struggle, triumph, and revelation. You'll see how ADHD, often perceived as a hindrance, became a unique lens through which I viewed the world, offering challenges and unexpected advantages.

This book is for anyone who has ever felt different, for those who have struggled to fit into the conventional mould, and for the silent warriors battling their minds every day. It's a reminder that success is not always a straight line.

The guidance in this book has been effective for me, but it may not be universally applicable to all individuals with ADHD, and some therapists may have different opinions. I hope this book serves as a helpful guide for those navigating this condition.

Annamaria RZ

Chapter One

Before School

You might find it surprising if I told you that I am an adult with ADHD. Despite this challenge, I have managed to achieve a high level of education. But to truly understand my journey, we must start from the very beginning, my childhood. It is there, in the early, chaotic days of my youth, that the story begins.

The morning sun filtered through the lace curtains, casting delicate patterns on the worn wooden floor. I sat cross-legged on the carpet, my toys arranged in perfect symmetry, just as Mama liked it. Everything had its place, and there was no room for disorder in our home.

Mama's voice echoed from the kitchen, sharp and insistent, as she berated me for leaving a single crayon out of its box the night before.

"Why can't you ever do anything right?" she snapped, her words stinging more than any physical blow could. I hung my head, my small fingers fidgeting with the hem of my dress, trying to make myself invisible. Mama's world was one of precision and control, and any deviation was met with her relentless criticism.

Mama had her moments, though. Sometimes she would disappear into her room for days, the door firmly shut, leaving me with Grandma. Those were the times I dreaded most. Grandma's house was a stark contrast to our meticulously kept home. It was filled with the scent of incense and the heavy presence of religious icons staring down from every wall.

Grandma was a woman of faith, devout and unyielding. She believed in the omnipresence of God and the inherent sinfulness of mankind. According to her, every mistake was a mark against my soul, an indication of my unworthiness in the eyes of the Almighty.

"God does not like naughty children," she would say sternly, "You must repent for your bad behaviour."

I spent countless hours in the dimly lit church, the air thick with the scent of burning candles and old wood. The sermons were long and incomprehensible to my five-year-old mind. I would sit there, bored and restless, my legs swinging beneath the pew, longing to be anywhere else. Grandma's gaze would fall on me, a silent reminder to behave, to repent.

At home, I lived under the weight of Mama's compulsions. Every room had to be spotless, every object in its rightful place. I learned to move quietly, to make myself small and unobtrusive, hoping to avoid her anger.

Mama's moods were like storms, sudden and unpredictable, leaving destruction in their wake. And in those moments, I was left to navigate the sea of my childhood alone.

One day, as I sat in the living room, carefully aligning my toys, Mama's voice cut through the silence.

"Why do you always make such a mess?" she demanded, her eyes blazing with frustration. I flinched, my heart pounding in my chest.

"I'm sorry, Mama," I whispered, my voice barely audible.

"Sorry isn't good enough," her fingers gripping my shoulder with a force that made me wince, "You need to learn to do things right. God knows I've tried to teach you."

The guilt and shame were my constant companions. I internalised her words, believing that I was fundamentally flawed and incapable of meeting her exacting standards. I began to associate my self-worth with my ability to maintain order and follow the rigid rules she imposed.

The visits to Grandma's were no reprieve. There, I was reminded of my moral failings and my need for divine forgiveness. The church became a place of penance rather than solace, a reminder of my shortcomings.

"You must pray for forgiveness," Grandma would say, her hands clasped tightly around her rosary, "Only then will you find redemption."

But the prayers felt hollow, the words empty. I didn't understand what I was asking forgiveness for. I was a child, yearning for love and acceptance, but finding only judgement and condemnation. My self-esteem withered under relentless scrutiny, and my confidence eroded by the constant criticism.

The days blurred into weeks, the weeks into months, each one marked by the weight of expectations I could never quite meet. Mama's anger, Grandma's disappointment, the oppressive atmosphere of the church—it all melded into a suffocating blanket, leaving me gasping for breath.

———————————————————————————————

One day, my older cousin brought a ping-pong ball to Grandma's house. He played with it, throwing it forcefully onto the ground. The ball produced a lovely sound that I had never heard before. I watched him with great interest and asked if he would give me the ball, as I wanted to play with it.

But he refused, saying, "You're just a child and will destroy it." He continued to play in front of me, unfazed by my request.

Three days later, to my astonishment, I saw that Grandpa had brought a cardboard box, carefully arranged with numerous ping-pong balls. I wondered to myself, "How did Grandpa know that I love them?" Grateful and curious, I followed him. He placed the box on the table in Grandma's kitchen and left the house again. I wondered why he hadn't given the balls directly to me. Perhaps he wanted to surprise me with them?

I thought that it would be no problem if I grabbed two of the balls to play with and then put them back in the box afterward. I loved the sound they made when they hit the ground. I wondered if they might make different, interesting sounds if they knocked against the wall. I couldn't wait, so I quickly picked up two of the balls and threw them at the clean kitchen wall. As I had imagined, the balls produced a different sound upon hitting the wall. However, to my surprise, they had suddenly burst open, their yolks splattered all over the room.

At that moment, I realised my mistake: the "ping-pong balls" were eggs. The sound of them bursting had alerted Grandma, who came up from the basement, her face a mix of anger and disbelief. She scolded me harshly, her words sharp and unforgiving. I stood there, feeling the weight of my error, the remains of the eggs still dripping down the kitchen walls.

In some quiet moments, when the house was still and the shadows grew long, I would retreat into my mind, crafting stories of escape and adventure. In my imagination, I was strong and capable, free from the chains of my reality. I was battling unseen foes and emerging victorious.

Those fantasies were my sanctuary, a place where I could be anything I wanted, unbound by the expectations of others. They were a glimpse of a future where I was more than just a collection of flaws and failures—a future where I could rise above the limitations imposed upon me and forge my path.

———-----------------------

One sweltering summer afternoon, I wandered into Grandma's garden, seeking refuge from the atmosphere of the house. The garden was a wild, tangled place, a stark contrast to the rigid order inside. Here, I could lose myself in the chaotic beauty of overgrown plants and the buzzing of insects.

As I explored, I noticed a large, shiny beetle scuttling across the stone path. Fascinated by its iridescent shell and determined to capture it, I reached for the nearest object—a delicate, handcrafted mug Grandma treasured. Carefully, I placed the mug over the beetle, hoping to trap it, but as I lifted the mug to peek underneath, the beetle darted out. In my panic, I dropped the mug. It shattered into countless pieces, the sound echoing throughout the garden.

My heart sank. The mug was one of Grandma's prized possessions, a gift from her mother. The vibrant colours and intricate patterns that once adorned its surface now lay in a heap of broken shards. I stood frozen, a cold dread creeping over me as I heard Grandma's footsteps approaching.

"What have you done?" she cried, her voice a mixture of shock and anger. She knelt by the broken pieces, her hands trembling as she picked them up. "This was my favourite mug. How could you be so careless?"

Tears welled up in my eyes as I struggled to find the words, "I'm sorry, Grandma," I whispered, my voice choking with guilt and fear, "I didn't mean to break it. I just wanted to catch the beetle."

Grandma's eyes, usually stern, now brimmed with disappointment, "You need to be more careful, child. You can't just go around breaking things. This was very important to me, and now it's gone because of your thoughtlessness."

Her words cut deep, leaving scars on my already fragile self-esteem. I wanted to explain, to make her understand that I never intended to cause harm, but the weight of my mistake was too heavy. All I could do was promise, over and over, that I would never do it again.

The rest of the day passed in a haze of remorse. Grandma's reprimands echoed in my mind, mingling with the constant criticism from Mama. It felt as though every misstep, every small error, was further proof of my inadequacy.

—--

A week later, I spotted another big beetle in the garden. I couldn't resist myself; I grabbed my grandmother's hat, delicately placed it on the beetle, and carefully scooped it up with a small piece of newspaper. Securing it in a tiny can, I tucked it into my shirt pocket.

The next day, my grandmother took me to church. As the priest droned on with his sermon, I found myself growing increasingly bored. Unable to resist the temptation, I quietly retrieved the beetle from my pocket, careful not to attract attention.

But as luck would have it, just as I let the beetle crawl onto my hand, it slipped from my grasp and scuttled away. Panic surged through me and I watched in horror as it disappeared under the pew in front of us. Moments later, the elderly woman sitting in front of me let out a piercing shriek.

"There's a bug on me!" she cried, frantically trying to shake something off her dress. Congregation members around her jumped up, alarmed by her distress.

My grandmother's eyes widened as she turned to me. "Is that beetle yours?" she whispered.

I nodded, eyes stinging with tears. "I'm sorry, Grandma," I murmured, feeling like the smallest child in the world.

After what felt like an eternity of embarrassment and scolding, the beetle was finally captured and released outside by a helpful church volunteer. The service resumed, but the atmosphere had changed. People cast sideways glances at me, and I couldn't help but feel the weight of their judgement.

On the way home, my grandmother kept a tight grip on my hand. "You must learn to control your impulses, dear," she said firmly, "And we need to respect other people's spaces, especially in church."

———

Grandma caught a common cold that lingered for days, causing her to reach for her trusty Dozenget tablets. She kept them in a drawer in her room, and as she busied herself in the kitchen making chicken soup, I went to sneak a peek.

Cautiously, I slipped into her room and approached the drawer. The box of Dozenget tablets sat right on top, with trembling fingers, I opened the box and retrieved a single tablet.

I stared at it for a moment, feeling a rush of guilt but also a tingling excitement. I wanted to see what it tasted like. Without another thought, I popped the tablet into my mouth. The taste was surprisingly sweet, a burst of fruity flavour that I hadn't expected. It was delicious, unlike anything I had ever tasted before.

Unable to resist, I quickly closed the box and retreated to my room, trying to ignore the gnawing guilt in the pit of my stomach. Minutes passed, and the taste of the first tablet still lingered on my tongue. The temptation was too strong. The tablets were incredibly delicious, and I couldn't resist taking more from the box.

One after another, I chewed and ate about five of them. When I noticed the box was nearly empty, I stopped and quickly left the scene. About an hour later, my face and body were covered in red rashes.

I felt an insufferable itching all over my body and began to cry. When Grandma saw me, she was awestruck, her eyes wide with shock and concern. She rushed to my side, her earlier anger replaced with worry, and tried to calm me down while figuring out what had happened.

She speculated that perhaps a dangerous mosquito had bitten me or that I had contracted a horrible disease. In a panic, she took me to the emergency room. The doctor diagnosed it as an allergic reaction, but neither he nor Grandma could determine what had caused it.

——
——————

I remember the day I first saw Grandma's old desk alarm clock. It sat on the corner of her oak desk, its bronze frame tarnished with age but still ticking away with a steady rhythm. The sound of it fascinated me, a steady tick-tock that never stopped.

The clock was unlike any other I had seen before—small, with intricate engravings around the face, and hands that moved with a peculiar smoothness. I couldn't take my eyes off it. What made it tick? How did it know the time? My mind buzzed with questions that I knew I needed to answer. And that's when the idea struck me. I would open it up and see for myself.

In the dim light of Grandma's study, while she napped in the next room, I crept up to the desk. The can opener I had sneaked from the kitchen felt cold and awkward in my hand, but I was determined. I placed the clock on its back, hesitating only for a second before I pressed the blade to the metal casing.

The first twist was the hardest. The metal was old and stubborn, but I felt a thrill as it gave way. It wasn't like the neat, satisfying clicks of a regular can—no, this was messier, more chaotic.

The clock's insides began to spill out in a jumble of gears, springs, and tiny screws that rolled across the desk. My heart raced. I felt like an explorer, uncovering the hidden mechanisms of a strange and ancient artifact.

But as I pried the last bit of casing off, the thrill turned to panic. The once-ticking clock lay in pieces, its innards a tangle of metal and springs. I tried to piece it back together, my fingers fumbling with the unfamiliar parts, but it was no use. The clock was destroyed, and the ticking had stopped.

I stared at the mess I had made, my heart sinking. I hadn't just stopped the clock; I had ended its life, the steady rhythm that had filled the room now replaced by a heavy silence. I felt guilt and fear, knowing that Grandma would soon wake up and find her beloved clock in ruins.

But at that moment, amidst the wreckage, I felt something else too—a strange sense of accomplishment. I had wanted to know how it worked, and now I did. The clock was no longer a mystery to me, even if it was now broken beyond repair.

That sense of curiosity, the need to understand and explore, had driven me to this moment.

It was a bittersweet victory, one that I knew would come with consequences. But as I stared down at the remains of the clock, I couldn't help but feel a small, secret thrill.

However, it didn't take much for Grandma to notice something was wrong. She must have sensed it—the absence of that familiar, comforting sound. I heard her footsteps approaching from the other room, and my heart pounded in my chest.

The door creaked open, and there she was, her eyes immediately falling on the chaos that was once her clock. Her face paled, and for a moment, she just stared, as if unable to process what she was seeing. Then she looked at me, her eyes filled with a mixture of shock and disbelief.

"Elizabeth," she whispered, her voice trembling, "What have you done?"

I opened my mouth to speak, to explain, but the words caught in my throat. What could I say? That I was curious? That I wanted to see how it worked?!

Grandma slowly approached the desk, her hand reaching out to touch the twisted remains of the clock. Her fingers hovered over the gears and springs, her expression sorrowful, "This clock... It was my father's. He gave it to me before he passed away."

"I'm so sorry, Grandma," I managed to choke out, "I didn't mean to... I just wanted to see how it worked."

She closed her eyes, taking a deep breath. "Curiosity is a powerful thing," she said softly, "But sometimes, it leads us to places we can't come back from."

I nodded, wiping away the tears that had begun to spill down my cheeks, "I didn't know it was so important to you."

She finally sat down at the desk, her hand resting on the broken clock, "It's not about the clock, dear. It's about understanding the consequences of our actions. You're smart, Elizabeth—too smart for your own good sometimes, but with that intelligence comes responsibility. You have to think before you act, to consider what might happen if things go wrong."

She wasn't yelling or punishing me, but her disappointment made me feel far worse. I wanted to make it right, to fix what I had broken, but I knew it was too late. The clock was beyond repair, and so was the trust I had broken.

When I was about six, I loved exploring my grandma's attic. It was like a treasure trove of old, forgotten things—dusty books, faded photographs, and mysterious boxes filled with who-knows-what.

One afternoon, I went up there just to take a quick look, but as always, I got completely lost in my own world. I remember finding an old trunk tucked away in a corner. It was filled with all sorts of oddities—old coins, brittle letters, and even a rusty key that I was sure unlocked something important.

Time slipped away without me noticing. I rifled through old clothes that smelled of mothballs, tried on a ridiculous feathered hat, and even spent what felt like hours just flipping through a yellowed photo album, imagining the lives of the people in the pictures. I was so engrossed that I didn't hear my grandma calling me for dinner, or even when she started yelling my name in a panic.

By the time I finally decided to go back downstairs, it was pitch black outside. As I opened the attic door, I was shocked to see police officers in the living room, along with a group of my grandma's neighbours. The whole house was in chaos. My grandma was pale and trembling, my mom was sobbing into her hands, and the neighbours were speaking in hushed, worried tones.

As soon as my grandma saw me at the top of the stairs, she let out a cry of relief and ran to hug me. "Where have you been?"

she cried, holding me so tight I could barely breathe, "We thought you were missing!"

Apparently, when they couldn't find me anywhere in the house or the yard, they feared the worst. My mom had come over as soon as she heard, and by the time the police arrived, they were already imagining all sorts of terrible scenarios. I felt terrible seeing my mom in tears, but at the same time, I couldn't quite understand what the fuss was about—I'd just been upstairs, lost in my own little adventure.

Chapter Two

School

I remember the first day of school vividly. I loved going to school, but I couldn't understand why I felt so anxious. The excitement and anxiety were almost too much to bear. The morning light streamed through the windows, casting a golden hue over my room. I fidgeted with my clothes, my mind racing with thoughts I couldn't control. My mom's voice was a distant murmur as they prepared breakfast downstairs.

When I arrived at the school, the building seemed enormous. Children clustered in groups, their laughter ringing through the air. I felt a pang of isolation, my heart pounding in my chest. My teacher, Mrs. Thompson, greeted me with a warm smile, but I could see the slight hesitation in her eyes. I had been labelled even before I set foot in the classroom.

The first few days were a blur. The constant hum of activity overwhelmed my senses. I struggled to sit still, my fingers drumming against the desk, my legs bouncing uncontrollably. Mrs. Thompson's voice seemed to fade in and out, the words slipping through my grasp like sand.

One afternoon, as we worked on a group project, I found myself lost in a swirl of thoughts. The other kids chatted easily, their ideas flowing seamlessly. I tried to contribute, but my thoughts came out jumbled, my words tangled. They looked at me with confusion and impatience. I wanted to explain, to make them understand, but I couldn't find the right words.

It was a bright, sunny morning when I decided that today would be different. I was tired of feeling out of place and misunderstood, so I set out to make my mark in primary school. My mind, always buzzing with thoughts and ideas, concocted a plan that seemed brilliant at the time.

During our math lesson, I grew restless. The numbers on the blackboard blurred together, and Mrs. Thompson's voice faded into the background. I glanced around the classroom, my eyes landing on the stack of colourful construction paper on the supply shelf. An idea sparked, and I couldn't resist.

When Mrs. Thompson turned her back to write on the board, I slipped out of my seat and quietly made my way to the supplies. I grabbed a handful of paper and scissors, sneaking back to my desk. My heart raced with excitement as I began to cut the paper into small shapes, oblivious to the problems we were supposed to be solving.

It wasn't long before my classmates noticed. Whispers spread through the room, and curious eyes watched as I crafted paper animals and folded tiny airplanes. One by one, my friends started to ask for the creations, and soon enough, my desk was surrounded by eager hands.

The commotion drew Mrs. Thompson's attention. She turned around, confused and frustrated, and demanded, "What is going on here?"

The room fell silent, all eyes on me. I tried to explain, my words tumbling out in a rush, "I just thought... Maybe we could make something fun for a change. The math was getting boring."

But the damage was done. My inattentiveness and impulsivity had disrupted the class, and Mrs. Thompson was disappointed. She confiscated the paper and scissors, directing everyone back to their seats, and tried to hide her anger and appear calm. I guiltily slumped down in my chair.

Many sunny days passed by the windows as we learned in our classrooms. Mrs.

Thompson's voice droned on, blending with the hum of the overhead fan, creating a lullaby of monotony that made the minutes drag.

I shifted in my seat at the back of the class, desperately trying to stay focused on the multiplication tables she was reciting. But my attention kept wandering, fixated on the elaborate braids of the two girls sitting in front of me. Their intricate hairstyles seemed to weave a mesmerising dance, and an idea began to take shape in my restless mind.

I glanced around to make sure Mrs. Thompson's back was turned, then reached forward with a mischievous grin. My fingers worked quickly, knotting the ends of the girls' braids together in a delicate tangle. I bit my lip, stifling a giggle as I imagined their confusion.

The bell for recess finally rang, breaking the spell of the lesson. The two girls stood up simultaneously, and the instant their braids pulled tight, chaos erupted. Gasps and giggles filled the room as they struggled to free themselves from the unexpected knot.

Mrs. Thompson, her sharp gaze cutting through the commotion, marched over with a stormy expression. Her eyes landed on the tangled girls, then shifted to me. I tried to hide my grin, but it was no use.

"Elizabeth!" the teacher's voice cut through the noise like a knife, "What on earth are you doing?"

The room fell silent. I looked down at my desk, feeling my cheeks flush, "Just having a bit of fun, Mrs. Thompson," I mumbled, trying to sound innocent.

Mrs. Thompson sighed, clearly frustrated, "Disrupting others is not acceptable. You need to focus on your work instead of causing trouble."

I nodded, my heart sinking as I realised I'd be spending recess in the classroom. But honestly, a little excitement was worth it. As Mrs. Thompson untangled the girls' braids, I let my mind wander again, dreaming of adventures beyond the dull confines of the room.

Despite the scolding, a tiny part of me felt triumphant. Boredom was my real enemy, and sometimes, a bit of mischief was the only way to keep it at bay.

———————————————————————————————

I remember one day specifically when we went on a field trip with our school to a historical museum. As usual, I couldn't stay focused on the tour guide's dull voice. My attention kept drifting to the exhibits—ancient artifacts, old paintings, and dusty relics from a time long gone.

At some point, while everyone else was huddled around a display case, I wandered off. I don't even remember making the decision to leave; one moment I was there, and the next, I was pushing open a creaky old door at the end of a dimly lit hallway.

I stepped inside, and the door closed behind me with a soft click. The room was dark, lit only by a small, dusty window high up on the wall. It was filled with all sorts of strange things—ancient maps, tattered books, and a few broken pieces of what looked like old machinery.

I started exploring, running my fingers over the dusty surfaces, but then something strange happened. The room felt like it was closing in on me, and the silence became almost unbearable.

Time seemed to stop. I don't know if it was minutes or hours, but the longer I stayed in that room, the more my imagination started to get the best of me. My heart began to race, and a terrifying thought crept into my mind: what if I was stuck in this room forever? What if no one ever found me?

I imagined myself sitting in the same spot, day after day, slowly becoming covered in dust, just like the artifacts surrounding me. I could almost see it—me, forgotten in this tiny, hidden room, my hair turning grey and cobwebs forming around my frozen body.

The idea that I could remain in this room for the rest of my life, unnoticed and alone, made my chest tighten with fear.

I started to panic. I ran to the door and tried to open it, but it wouldn't budge. My hands were trembling as I pounded on it, shouting for help, but my voice sounded small and insignificant in the vast emptiness of the museum. The walls seemed to close in even more, and I was sure I'd be lost forever.

Finally, after what felt like an eternity, the door creaked open. A flood of light from the hallway blinded me for a moment. There stood my frustrated teacher, "Where have you been?" she scolded, pulling me out of the room. I was too shaken to answer.

It turned out I hadn't been missing for long, but those moments in that room felt like a lifetime. Even now, I can still remember the feeling of that thick, suffocating dust, and the overwhelming fear that I might never be found. That experience left a lasting impression on me, a reminder of just how easily I can get lost—not just physically, but in my own mind, too.

———--

"Elizabeth, would you care to explain why you thought it appropriate to draw all over your maths notebook?"

Mrs. Fletcher, my other grade teacher, stood at the front of the classroom, her eyes fixed on me.

I glanced down at my desk, my cheeks burning. It had been a masterpiece, or so I thought—a swirling landscape of dragons, castles, knights and queens. But Mrs. Fletcher didn't see it that way.

"I got bored," I mumbled.

Boredom was my constant companion, a shadow that followed me everywhere. It whispered in my ear during history lessons, coaxing me to fidget and squirm, to tap my pencil against the desk until my classmates glared at me in annoyance. It nudged me during science class, urging me to doodle in the margins of my notebook instead of taking notes on the phases of the moon.

But boredom was only the beginning. My mind was a whirlwind, a chaotic storm that refused to settle. I often lost track of time, forgetting to hand in assignments or missing entire classes because I had wandered off somewhere, lost in a daydream.

One day, I was supposed to present a book report on "Charlotte's Web." I had read the book, and loved it even, but when the time came to stand in front of the class, my mind went blank. I stammered, trying to recall the plot, but all I could think about was the spider in the corner of the ceiling, spinning its delicate web. I ended up rambling about spiders for ten minutes before Mrs. Fletcher mercifully cut me off.

Then there were the endless mistakes with my homework. I often started my assignments with enthusiasm, only to get distracted halfway through. I would leave math problems unfinished, essays with missing paragraphs, and science projects half-built.

Once, I handed in a geography project to the wrong country. I had researched Brazil, only to realise the night before it was due that I was supposed to be reporting on Argentina. In my panic, I tried to switch the names in my report, but my teacher was not fooled.

Socially, I was a disaster. My impulsiveness got me into trouble more times than I could count. I blurted out whatever came to mind, often interrupting my friends and teachers. I once told my best friend, Sarah, that her new haircut made her look like a porcupine. I hadn't meant to be mean, but the words spilled out before I could stop them. She didn't speak to me for a week.

In gym class, I was always the last one picked for teams. I couldn't follow the rules, always forgetting which side I was supposed to be on or what the objective of the game was. During a soccer match, I once kicked the ball into our own goal, much to the dismay of my teammates. They shouted at me, their faces red with anger, but I just stood there, bewildered and embarrassed.

In the mornings, I was always disoriented and late. I scrambled to gather my things, stuffing my textbooks and notebooks haphazardly into my backpack. One day, I knew I was forgetting something, but the nagging feeling was drowned out by the rush of getting out the door.

Mrs. Fletcher's icy gaze met me as I entered the classroom, late as usual. "Elizabeth," she began, her tone dripping with exasperation, "Where is your homework?"

My heart sank. I had spent hours on that history essay, meticulously researching and writing about the French revolution. But there it was, sitting forlornly on my desk at home. "I forgot it," I whispered, my voice barely audible.

—---

Our middle school was huge and navigating the school hallways was like being trapped in a labyrinth. My mind wandered as I walked, imagining adventures and stories far more exciting than reality. One day, I was so engrossed in a daydream about exploring a secret garden that I completely missed my turn to answer a math equation.

I wandered the halls, my thoughts a tangled mess until the bell rang. Panic set in as I realised I had no idea where I was. By the time I found my way back, the class was halfway over, and Mrs. Fletcher was waiting for me, arms crossed and a frown on her face.

My mind jumps from one idea to the next. During a science group project, I misheard our assignment. While my group mates were building a model of the solar system, I was busy crafting an elaborate volcano.

When the day of the presentation arrived, I proudly placed my volcano next to their planets, only to be met with incredulous stares. "Elizabeth," one of my teammates said, "What are you doing? This isn't part of our project."

Sitting still was an impossible feat. My legs bounced under the desk, my fingers drummed incessantly, and I often found myself standing up in the middle of class without realising it. During a particularly quiet reading session, I couldn't resist the urge to tap my pencil rhythmically against my desk.

The sound echoed through the room, earning me glares from my classmates and a sharp reprimand from Mrs. Fletcher, "Elizabeth, if you can't sit still, you'll have to stand at the back of the class."

And so I stood, fidgeting even more, feeling the weight of everyone's eyes on me.

Sometimes I could not control myself and express my comments in the middle of the teacher's speech. I was famous for my disruptive comments.

During a geography lesson, Mrs. Fletcher was explaining the concept of time zones. Bored and restless, I blurted out, "Why can't we all just use the same time? It would be so much easier!"

The class erupted in laughter, and Mrs. Fletcher sighed deeply, "Please save your comments for after the lesson." But my thoughts had already drifted to another topic, my curiosity constantly pulling me in different directions.

—————————————————————

Sometimes, the classroom would be a battleground of restless energy. I sat at the back, struggling to stay at my desk while the noise and commotion swirled around me. The boys in my class were a whirlwind of chaos—loud, boisterous, and often challenging the limits of the teachers' patience.

Today, their antics seemed louder than usual. Ben and Tom, the ringleaders of mischief, had decided that today's lesson on history was the perfect backdrop for their latest game. Their whispered jokes and occasional bursts of laughter were like a magnet pulling me into their orbit.

I tried to focus on the lesson, but their energy was infectious. Every so often, their loud whispers would transform into full-blown giggles, drawing disapproving glances from Mrs. Wilson. She would sternly remind them to pay attention, but her warnings were like trying to hold back a wave with a surfboard.

I couldn't help but get caught up in their antics. When Ben threw a crumpled piece of paper at Tom, the immediate reaction was a volley of similar projectiles that ricocheted off desks and landed with a thud on the floor. My desk became an unintended target as a stray paper landed squarely in front of me. I picked it up, my curiosity piqued. It was a poorly drawn picture of Mrs. Wilson with horns and a devilish grin.

A smirk played on my lips as I glanced over at them. They caught my eye and grinned, clearly pleased with their handiwork. Unable to resist, I folded the paper into a paper aeroplane and launched it with a flick of my wrist. It soared across the room and landed with precision on Tom's desk.

Tom's eyes widened in surprise, and his laugh erupted like a firecracker. Mrs. Wilson's gaze snapped to our corner of the room, her expression a mix of irritation and disbelief. "Elizabeth! Is this how you're choosing to spend your time in my class?"

I swallowed hard, feeling the heat of her gaze. "Sorry, Mrs. Wilson," I muttered, though my voice lacked genuine remorse.

The thrill of the mischief lingered, even as I was summoned to the front of the class to face her stern reprimand. As I walked past Ben and Tom, their sympathetic smiles were almost comforting. They knew the game all too well, and their presence made me feel less alone in my misadventures. The punishment was predictable: a few minutes of extra work on my own, and a note to my parents about my behaviour.

The next day felt eerily similar to the day before. The sun streamed through the tall windows and Mrs. Collins was lecturing us on the basics of geography. Her voice blended into the hum of the fan above us, creating a monotonous drone.

I was seated at the back of the room, trying to stay focused yet again. Ben and Tom were as energetic as ever, their mischief was in full swing.

Ben had managed to smuggle a small rubber ball into the classroom, and he was tossing it softly to Tom, who caught it with exaggerated moves. Their silent game of catch drew more giggles than the lesson did, and their laughter was impossible to ignore.

I couldn't resist joining in. When Ben threw the ball in my direction, I caught it with a practised flick and tossed it back, grinning as Tom's eyes widened in surprise. We continued the game under the guise of paying attention, the rubber ball bouncing back and forth across the room.

The inevitable happened when Mrs. Collins turned to write on the board. The ball ricocheted off my desk and rolled across the floor, coming to a stop at Mrs. Collins' feet. Her eyes narrowed as she bent down to pick it up.

"Elizabeth!" Mrs. Collins' voice cut through the noise like a whip, "What is the meaning of this disruption?"

My heart sank as the room fell silent. I looked up, trying to suppress my nervous giggle. "Sorry," I said, though the thrill of the game still lingered.

Mrs. Collins sighed, her face showing irritation, "This behaviour is unacceptable. You need to learn to control your impulses and focus on the lesson. I expect more from you."

I nodded, suddenly feeling the sting of her words. As she turned to address the rest of the class, I slunk back in my seat, my cheeks flushed with embarrassment. Ben and Tom shot me sympathetic glances, their grins replaced by guilty looks.

With recess approaching, I was left behind to finish my extra assignment—an essay on why paying attention is important and a set of extra geography problems.

When the bell rang, the rush of students heading to the playground was a reminder of the lively world outside. I stayed behind, working through my tasks with a mix of determination and frustration. The playground sounds were a reminder of all the fun I was missing.

———————————————————————

Growing up, I always struggled with saying no. It wasn't that I didn't want to—I just couldn't. The words seemed to get stuck somewhere between my mind and my mouth, and by the time I found the courage to refuse, it was already too late. People knew this about me, and they used it to their advantage more times than I'd like to admit.

One of the earliest memories I have of being taken advantage of happened in middle school. I had just started at a new school, and making friends wasn't easy for me. My ADHD made it hard to focus on conversations, and I was always worried that I'd say something wrong or embarrassing. So when Emily, one of the popular girls, started talking to me, I felt like I'd won the lottery. I couldn't believe that someone like her would want to be my friend.

One day during lunch, Emily asked if she could borrow my homework. I hesitated, knowing that it was wrong, but she smiled at me in that way that made my heart race with anxiety.

"Come on, Elizabeth," she said, "You're so good at this stuff, and I'm really struggling. You don't want me to fail, do you?"

The truth was, I didn't. I didn't want her to fail, and I didn't want to lose her as a friend. So I handed over my homework, convincing myself that it was just this once, that it wasn't a big deal. But of course, it wasn't just that one time. It became a pattern, with Emily and others asking for my homework, my notes, my time—whatever they needed.

And every time, I gave in, feeling like I owed them something, like it was my responsibility to help.

Then there was the time in high school when I was paired with Mark for a group project. Mark was charming and charismatic, the kind of guy everyone liked. But he was also lazy. From the start, it was clear that he expected me to do all the work. He didn't even pretend to contribute; instead, he sweet-talked me, saying things like, "You're so much better at this than I am," and "I'd just mess it up if I tried."

I knew what was happening. I knew he was using me, but I didn't have the confidence to stand up to him. My self-esteem was so low that I believed I had to prove myself by doing all the work. So I did. I stayed up late, working on the project until my eyes burned, while Mark spent his time goofing off with his friends. And when we got an A, he took all the credit, leaving me with nothing but exhaustion and resentment.

There were countless other times when I was taken advantage of—when friends asked me to cover for them, to do things I didn't want to do, or to be there for them when they weren't there for me. I always felt like I owed them something, like I wasn't good enough on my own, so I gave and gave until there was nothing left.

It wasn't until much later, after years of therapy and learning more about my ADHD, that I realised how much I had been manipulated. My ADHD made it hard for me to set boundaries, to see when people were using me, and to have the confidence to stand up for myself.

Chapter Three

At Grandmother's Home

As I mentioned before, my grandma was deeply religious, her home was filled with religious icons, framed prayers, and the lingering scent of incense. She had a strict set of rules based on her faith, and any deviation was met with stern disapproval.

"Remember to say your prayers before bed," she would remind me, her voice firm but kind. Despite my best efforts, my mind would often wander during prayer time.

Adding to the challenge were my cousins, a trio of troublemakers who seemed to delight in making my life difficult. They thrived in the chaos they created, leaving a trail of messes wherever they went. I was often caught in the crossfire, their antics clashing with my attempts to find some semblance of order.

One summer day, we were all gathered at Grandma's for a family reunion. The house was bustling with relatives, the air thick with the smell of home-cooked food. My cousins were plotting their next prank. I tried to steer clear, knowing from experience that being near them usually meant trouble.

Despite my efforts, I couldn't avoid them for long. "Hey, Elizabeth," called Jack, the ringleader, "Come help us with something in the backyard."

Against my better judgement, I followed them, hoping this time would be different. They led me to the garden shed, their expressions innocent but their eyes gleaming with mischief. "We just need to get some tools for a project," said Lucy, the oldest, "Can you grab that paint can on the top shelf?"

As I reached for the can, they darted out of the shed, slamming the door behind them. I heard the lock click, trapping me inside. "Very funny, guys!" I shouted, pounding on the door. But they had already run off, laughing.

I finally managed to escape, only to find my cousins in the kitchen, covered in flour and giggling. The kitchen was a disaster zone—flour, sugar, and various baking ingredients scattered everywhere. Grandma stood in the doorway, her face a mask of shock and anger.

"Who did this?" she demanded, her eyes narrowing.

"Elizabeth did it," Lucy said quickly, pointing at me, "She wanted to bake cookies and made this mess."

"That's not true!" I protested, but my words fell on deaf ears. My cousins had already perfected their innocent looks, leaving me to shoulder the blame.

Grandma sighed, her disappointment palpable, "You know better than this. Clean up this mess immediately."

As I cleaned, my frustration grew. It seemed like no matter what I did, I couldn't escape the trouble my cousins caused. They knew I struggled to keep things in order, and they exploited that, framing me for their messes.

One afternoon, while everyone was gathered in the living room, Grandma realised her house keys were missing. She had a strict rule about where the keys should always be kept—on a hook by the door. My cousins had taken them and hidden them in the garden, but of course, they pointed the finger at me.

"Elizabeth was the last one near the door!"

"Yeah, she was looking at something on the hook!"

Grandma turned to me, her face serious, "Elizabeth, did you take the keys?"

"No, Grandma, I didn't!" I protested, my heart sinking as I realised I had no way to prove my innocence.

It took hours of searching before the keys were found buried under some leaves in the garden. By then, the damage was done. I could see the doubt in Grandma's eyes, even if she didn't say anything.

On another visit, a beautiful vase that had been in the family for generations was mysteriously broken. The sound of shattering glass had everyone rushing to the dining room. There stood my cousins, looking guilty but ready to place the blame.

"Elizabeth was playing with the vase earlier," Ben, the youngest, said quietly as if he was hesitant to accuse me.

"I wasn't! I was reading in the other room!" I exclaimed, feeling the familiar frustration rising.

But my cousins had planned it well. They had seen to it that no one else was around to confirm my alibi. Grandma looked at the broken pieces with a sigh, "Accidents happen, Elizabeth, but you need to be more careful."

Another evening, after Grandma had baked a batch of her famous chocolate chip cookies, a whole tray went missing. My cousins, with crumbs still on their faces, pointed at me.

"Elizabeth took the cookies and hid them," Lucy said with a smirk.

I was furious, "I didn't touch them! They did it!"

But with my reputation already tarnished by previous incidents, my protests seemed hollow. Grandma simply asked me to help bake a new batch, her disappointment evident.

During a family painting day, a can of paint was knocked over, splattering across the floor and walls. I was in another room getting more supplies, but my cousins blamed me once again.

I returned to find the mess and everyone staring at me, "I wasn't even here when it happened!"

Despite my pleas, the evidence—or rather, the lack of any defence—was against me. I ended up cleaning the mess while my cousins snickered from the sidelines.

On a day when we were all supposed to be doing our homework, my cousins concocted a plan to hide their incomplete assignments and blame me for taking them. When our parents asked for the homework, they all pointed to me.

"Elizabeth took our homework and hid it," Ben said, tears welling up in his eyes for added effect.

"But why would I do that? I have my homework to finish!" I argued, but it was no use.

Grandma, trying to be fair but tired of the constant drama, decided we all had to redo our assignments from scratch. My cousins grinned, knowing they'd successfully diverted attention from their laziness.

One particularly cunning trick involved a prank phone call to Grandma, made from her phone when she wasn't looking. They called a neighbour and pretended to be her, making absurd requests and causing confusion.

When the neighbour called back to ask about the strange conversation, my cousins reported, "Elizabeth was playing with the phone earlier."

Grandma looked incredibly upset, "Elizabeth, prank calls are not a joke."

"But it wasn't me!" I insisted, feeling helpless.

Chapter Four

Highschool

High school was supposed to be a fresh start, a chance to leave behind the chaos of middle school and prove that I could handle the demands of a more rigorous academic environment. But ADHD had other plans for me.

The first week was a whirlwind of new faces and new routines. I struggled to keep up with my schedule, often finding myself in the wrong classroom or forgetting which textbooks I needed for which class. It became a running joke among my peers—"Where's Elizabeth today?" they'd laugh, half expecting to find me in the janitor's closet instead of chemistry.

The workload was intense. Every class seemed to have a never-ending stream of assignments and projects. I tried to keep track, really I did. I bought a planner and set reminders on my phone, but it never seemed to be enough.

One evening, I stayed up late, determined to finish my biology project on cell structures. Exhaustion eventually took over, and I fell asleep at my desk, the diagrams half-drawn. The next morning, in my rush, I left the project behind. When Mrs. Blake asked for our projects, I felt a familiar sinking feeling. "I forgot it," I repeated, my voice a defeated whisper.

———------------------------------

High school was a minefield of social interactions. My impulsiveness made it hard to fit in. I often interrupted conversations, my thoughts spilling out unfiltered. During lunch one day, I accidentally knocked over a friend's tray while gesturing wildly, sending food splattering across the table.

"Elizabeth!" she exclaimed, her tone a mix of shock and frustration. I apologised profusely, but the damage was done.

Parties and social gatherings were equally daunting. The noise and chaos overwhelmed me, making it hard to focus on any one conversation. I would find

myself drifting from group to group, never quite fitting in, always feeling like an outsider looking in.

Tests were a nightmare. Sitting still for hours, focusing on a single task—it felt like torture. My mind would wander, my legs would jitter, and I'd find myself staring at the clock, willing the minutes to pass faster.

During a particularly important math exam, I realised halfway through that I had spent too much time on the first few problems and now had only minutes left to finish the rest.

Panic set in. My breathing quickened, my hands shook, and I quickly scribbled answers, hoping something would be right.

When the bell rang, I handed in my paper with a sinking heart, knowing I had done poorly.

I lost things constantly. My locker was a disaster zone, a jumble of books, papers, and random items. One day, I misplaced my chemistry textbook, only to find it weeks later under a pile of clothes in my bedroom. My teachers grew accustomed to my frantic searches for missing assignments and the look of defeat when I had to admit I'd lost something important yet again.

Despite the constant distractions and impulsive behaviour, my intelligence shone through in unexpected ways. In first grade, while other kids were learning to read basic words, I devoured chapter books.

My teacher, Mrs. Thompson, noticed my advanced reading level and encouraged me to explore more challenging material. "Elizabeth," she said one day, her eyes twinkling with pride, "You have a remarkable gift. Your reading comprehension is years ahead of your peers."

During a maths lesson, while my classmates struggled with simple addition, I grasped the concept of multiplication effortlessly. Numbers fascinated me, and I often found myself daydreaming about complex mathematical problems.

My third-grade teacher, Mr. Harris once said, "You have a mind for numbers that I've rarely seen at your age. It's a shame you find it so hard to focus."

As I moved into middle school, my intellect continued to outpace my peers. In science class, I absorbed information like a sponge, always eager to learn more about the natural world. My curiosity led me to ask questions that even stumped my teachers at times. Mrs. Carter, my seventh-grade science teacher, often told me, "Elizabeth, you have the potential to be a brilliant scientist. If only you could control that restless mind of yours."

During a school-wide quiz competition. I was part of the academic team, and despite my tendency to lose focus, my knowledge and quick thinking helped us win first place.

In English class, I wrote vivid, intricate tales that transported my readers to different worlds. Mrs. Wallace, my English teacher, once read one of my stories aloud to the class, saying, "Your storytelling is genius and a great example for others."

High school presented new challenges, but also opportunities to showcase my intellectual gifts. In advanced placement classes, I thrived on the complex material. My teachers often marvelled at my ability to grasp difficult concepts quickly. In physics, I understood theories and equations that left many of my classmates bewildered.

Physics and chemistry became my sanctuaries, the subjects were where my high IQ truly shone. The intricate dance of atoms and molecules, the elegance of physical laws—they captivated me. My teachers, Mr. Clark and Mrs. Patel, quickly recognized my talent. However, my enthusiasm often got the better of me.

In chemistry class, Mrs. Patel would begin writing a complex equation on the board, and before she could finish, I would blurt out the solution.

"Ethanol and oxygen react to form carbon dioxide and water!" I'd exclaim. My classmates would groan in unison, annoyed by my interruptions.

Mrs. Patel would smile, a mix of pride and exasperation. "Elizabeth, you're correct, but please give others a chance to think," she'd say gently, but it was hard to contain myself when the answers came so effortlessly.

Physics class was no different. Mr. Clark would pose a challenging problem, and my hand would shoot up before he even finished speaking. "The acceleration due to gravity is 9.8 metres per second squared!" I'd declare, cutting through the silence of the classroom.

My classmates' frustration was palpable. They would mutter under their breath, some rolling their eyes. "Elizabeth, give it a rest," someone would inevitably say. But I couldn't help it; the thrill of solving problems, of seeing the patterns and relationships, was intoxicating.

One day, Mr. Clark decided to challenge me. He wrote a particularly difficult problem on the board, one that stumped even the best students. "Let's see if you can solve this one," he said with a knowing smile.

I stared at the board, my mind racing. The problem was intricate, requiring a deep understanding of multiple physics concepts. For a moment, doubt crept in. But then, the pieces fell into place. "The answer is 42.7 Joules," I announced confidently.

Mr. Clark's smile widened, "Correct, but next time Elizabeth let's give everyone a chance to try."

The class erupted in groans and laughter, but I couldn't suppress the pride that swelled within me. Despite their annoyance, my classmates couldn't deny my talent. Slowly, some began to see beyond the interruptions and recognize my passion.

Outside of class, I formed study groups with those who shared my interest in science. We would spend hours discussing theories, solving problems, and exploring concepts far beyond the curriculum. In those moments, I felt truly understood and appreciated.

But it wasn't just about showing off or being the first to answer. Physics and chemistry gave me a sense of control and clarity that I rarely found elsewhere. The rules were fixed, and the outcomes were predictable. In a mind constantly swirling with thoughts and distractions, these subjects were my anchor, grounding me in their logic and precision.

Chapter Five

At Home

While school was a battleground of brilliance and distraction, home was another story entirely. My mom's obsessive nature and periods of depression cast a long shadow over our household. She was meticulous about cleanliness and order, an expectation that clashed violently with my ADHD-fueled chaos.

"Elizabeth, why can't you keep your room clean?" she'd exclaim, standing in the doorway of my bedroom. My room was a testament to my scatterbrained existence—books and papers strewn everywhere, art supplies left out, half-finished projects littering the floor.

"I'll clean it, Mom, I promise," I'd say, but the promises often went unfulfilled. My intentions were good, but the follow-through was a constant struggle.

Her periods of depression were even more challenging. During those times, she would retreat into herself, leaving me to navigate my world alone. When she emerged, it was often with a barrage of blame.

"Why can't you be more responsible? More like your cousins ?" she'd say, comparing me to my cousins who seemed to have inherited none of my struggles.

Her words stung, reinforcing the sense that my ADHD was a burden, a flaw that I couldn't escape. I wanted to please her, to be the daughter she deserved, but it felt like an impossible task. My mind simply didn't work the way she wanted it to.

Everyday routines were a constant battleground. My mom had a strict schedule for everything—mealtimes, homework, chores. But my ADHD made sticking to a routine incredibly difficult. I would get lost in a book or a drawing, completely forgetting about dinner time or the chore list pinned to the fridge.

"Elizabeth, how many times do I have to tell you to do your chores?" her voice edged with irritation, "Why can't you just remember?"

"I try, Mom, I do," I'd respond, feeling the weight of her disappointment. But trying didn't seem to be enough.

Arguments were frequent and often intense. My mom couldn't understand why I struggled with tasks that seemed so simple to her.

Her depression sometimes made her words harsher. "Do you even care about this family?" she once shouted during an argument, "Or are you just too wrapped up in your little world?"

Those words cut deep, leaving me feeling isolated and misunderstood. I did care, deeply, but expressing that was a constant challenge.

Chapter Six

The Struggle for Focus

During the day, it seemed like everything around me was designed to pull my attention away from my studies. The sound of birds chirping outside my window, the distant hum of cars passing by, even the creaking of the house as it settled—all of it was enough to derail my focus.

I would sit at my desk, textbooks open in front of me, and my mind would wander to the most random places. I'd start thinking about the shape of the clouds, the way the sunlight hit the floor, or a conversation I'd overheard in the hallway at school. Before I knew it, hours had passed, and I'd barely made a dent in my homework.

It was frustrating, but no matter how hard I tried, I couldn't make my brain stay on track. It was as if my mind was a kite, and the wind of distractions kept pulling it in different directions, making it impossible to keep it tethered to the ground. My ADHD made it almost unbearable to concentrate during the day, with so many stimuli fighting for my attention.

But at night, everything changed. When the house was quiet, and the world outside had gone to sleep, I found a strange peace. The distractions that plagued me during the day faded away, replaced by a comforting silence. The darkness wrapped around me like a blanket, and for the first time all day, my mind stopped racing. It was just me, the soft glow of my desk lamp, and the open pages of my textbooks.

I had discovered this almost by accident one night when I couldn't sleep. I wandered into the living room, the only sound was the soft ticking of the clock on the wall. I picked up my textbook out of boredom, but as I started reading, I realised something amazing—I could actually focus. The words on the page made sense, and I found myself absorbing the material in a way that had seemed impossible during the day. It was as if the quiet night had unlocked a part of my brain that had been shut off, allowing me to learn in a way that felt natural.

From that night on, I made a habit of studying late, when the world was still. It wasn't ideal, but it worked. I could get through chapters, finish assignments, and actually retain information, something that was almost impossible during the chaotic hours of daylight. It became my secret weapon, a way to manage my ADHD without the constant battle against distractions.

However, my parents didn't see it that way.
To them, my nocturnal study sessions were
a sign that something was wrong. They
didn't understand why I couldn't study
during the day like everyone else, why I had
to stay up late into the night when I should
be resting. They thought I was being
irresponsible, that I was neglecting my
studies during the day and only cramming
at night because I wasn't disciplined
enough.

The arguments started slowly at first—a concerned comment here, a gentle reminder there—but they quickly escalated into full-blown confrontations. My parents would find me at my desk, hunched over my books at two in the morning, and they'd demand to know why I wasn't sleeping, why I wasn't studying during the day. I tried to explain, to tell them that the quiet of the night was the only time I could truly focus, but they didn't understand. They thought I was making excuses, that I was just avoiding my responsibilities.

The worst part was that I couldn't even fully explain it to myself. Why couldn't I just study like everyone else? Why did I have to wait until the rest of the world was asleep to get anything done? It felt like my brain was wired differently, like I was fighting a battle no one else could see.

I had always dreamed of going to university, and when I received my acceptance letter, it felt like a victory, a testament to my hard work and determination. I had chosen life science, a field that fascinated me with its complexities and mysteries. The idea of delving into the intricacies of life was exhilarating. But as I began my studies, the reality of university life set in, and I realised that the journey was far more challenging than I had anticipated.

Every day, I would find a quiet corner in the library or my room, determined to focus and absorb the wealth of information before me. I would open my textbooks with great enthusiasm, but it was as if the world conspired against my concentration. A creaking chair, the faint rustle of a page turning, even the distant hum of the air conditioner seemed to break my focus. Each distraction, no matter how minor, felt like a wall being built between me and my studies.

Sitting down to study required a monumental effort. I'd start with the best intentions, only to find that after just a few minutes, my mind would drift. Thoughts would flutter from one idea to another—an upcoming social event, a conversation I had earlier, or even a stray word in the text that reminded me of something entirely unrelated. My brain seemed to operate in a constant state of flux, making it difficult to settle on a single thought for more than a moment.

Hours would pass, and I'd be exhausted from the mental gymnastics. I could spend an entire afternoon trying to get through a single paragraph, only to find that my understanding was still shaky.

It was disheartening. Each time I finally closed my textbook, I felt drained, as though the act of studying had sapped my energy reserves.

I envied my friends, who seemed to navigate their studies with ease. They could sit for hours in the library, deeply engrossed in their work, while I struggled to maintain focus for even a fraction of that time. They would breeze through chapters, while I felt like I was wading through molasses.

At first, I thought my inability to focus was just a matter of willpower. Perhaps I wasn't disciplined enough or lacked the right study habits. But as time went on, I began to question if there was something more to it. I started to wonder if there was something fundamentally different about the way my mind worked, something that made focusing and studying a constant battle.

The endless cycle of trying to study, getting distracted, and feeling drained left me feeling frustrated and isolated. I struggled to understand why this was so hard for me while it seemed effortless for others. I didn't know if it was a problem I could fix or just a part of who I was. All I knew was that I wanted to succeed, to prove that despite these challenges, I could excel in my studies.

Chapter Seven

The Classroom Struggle

The lecture hall was packed, the air thick with the murmur of students settling into their seats. The professor began his lecture on cellular biology, his voice a steady stream of information. I forced myself to sit up straight, focusing intently on every word he said. This was important—my future depended on understanding these concepts. I took deep breaths, trying to anchor myself in the moment.

For the first few minutes, I managed to hold onto my focus. The information about cell structures and functions seemed to sink in, and I scribbled notes furiously, determined to keep up. But then, like a sudden breeze scattering leaves, my concentration started to waver.

The professor's words became a distant hum as I stared at my notebook, the once-clear notes now blurring into a sea of unintelligible scribbles. My mind wandered further into a daydream, a place where the boundaries of reality and imagination blurred. I imagined myself as a scientist making groundbreaking discoveries, but the dream was fleeting and interrupted by the reality of my wandering attention.

I glanced around the room, seeing other students who seemed completely absorbed in the lecture. Their unwavering focus only served to grow my frustration. Why was it so difficult for me to concentrate?

The energy it took to fight off distractions felt like a constant drain. I could only maintain my focus for about five minutes before the wave of distraction crashed over me.

There were rare moments, though, when everything changed. When the topic was something I was deeply passionate about—genetics, for instance—I found myself in a state of intense concentration. My focus became so sharp that the world around me seemed to vanish. I would lose track of time, absorbing every detail, captivated

by the subject matter. It was an exhilarating escape from the constant struggle of everyday focus.

But those moments of profound engagement were exceptions rather than the norm. The confusion of having such a powerful reaction to certain subjects, while struggling so much with others, left me disoriented.

It made me question if there was something fundamentally wrong with me, or if I was simply trying to navigate a world that wasn't designed for my way of thinking.

Chapter Eight

The Exam taking

The weeks leading up to the university exams were a blur of frantic studying and mounting pressure. The library had become my second home, a sanctuary where I tried to immerse myself in the vast sea of information I needed to absorb.

I would sit at my desk, surrounded by piles of textbooks, notebooks, and scribbled notes. The walls of my study space were plastered with sticky notes and diagrams, each a visual reminder of what I needed to remember. Despite my best efforts, it felt like my mind was a sieve, with important details slipping through every time I got distracted. The process of studying was draining; I'd often spend hours attempting to get through a single chapter, only to find myself having made little progress.

The smallest things could pull me away from my studies. The ticking of the clock seemed louder than usual, each second a reminder of how much time I felt was slipping away. A faint smell of coffee from the café downstairs would make me long for a break, and the distant chatter of students walking past would disrupt my train of thought. Even a stray word or phrase in my textbook could trigger a cascade of unrelated thoughts, pulling me into a daydream that was hard to escape.

My irritation would increase as the days went by. Despite my good intentions, I would find that I had only managed to cover half of a textbook, and sometimes even less. My notes were filled with fragmented ideas and incomplete thoughts. Each time I looked at the clock, I felt a pang of anxiety, knowing that it was ticking down to the exam days.

The day of the first exam arrived, and the pressure was palpable. I walked into the exam hall with a mix of anxiety and determination. My preparation had been a constant battle with distraction, but I hoped that my innate understanding of the material would see me through. As the exam paper was handed out, I felt a rush of adrenaline, excitement, and dread.

Sitting down to tackle the questions, I found myself facing the fruits of my labour. The material I had managed to study came flooding back, and I could see that some of it was still fresh in my mind. However, other parts felt like they were locked away and inaccessible. I tried to channel the intense focus I had experienced with my favourite subjects, but it was a difficult task. The distractions of the past weeks lingered, making it hard to concentrate on the exam questions.

During multiple-choice tests, I had developed a troubling habit. If I encountered a question I wasn't entirely sure about, I would leave it unanswered and mark it for later. However, my tendency to get easily distracted meant that when I moved on to the next question, I often forgot which questions I had intended to revisit. I would sometimes mark the answer to a subsequent question in the space of the one I had left blank, a chain reaction that led to multiple errors.

The confusion didn't stop there. In the frenzy of flipping through pages, I would occasionally miss questions on the back of the test paper entirely. The sense of panic would set in when I realised, too late, that I had skipped several questions. The realisation that I had made avoidable mistakes left me feeling frustrated and self-critical.

After the exams, my mood would plummet. I would replay the test in my mind, anguishing over each mistake. The realisation that my careless errors had cost me valuable marks was a heavy blow to my self-esteem.

The knowledge that I had inadvertently sabotaged my own efforts because of my distractions was deeply upsetting. I would be left questioning my competence, and the pressure to perform better seemed to build up even more.

It was clear that I needed to find ways to better manage my concentration and energy if I wanted to achieve my full potential.

————————————————————————

The exam results arrived and as I opened the envelope, a wave of disappointment washed over me. The grades I had earned were a far cry from the level of excellence I had hoped to achieve. My performance, while enough to pass, did not reflect the effort I had poured into my studies. The discrepancy between my results and my expectations was jarring.

The disappointment was compounded by the reactions of those around me. In the bustling corridors of the university, I could hear whispers and muffled laughter, always just out of reach.

Some classmates made cruel jokes about my performance, their comments laced with mockery. They thought I was slacking off, spending my time on frivolous activities rather than studying. Their words stung as much as my failures.

Others, who were more aware of my struggles, viewed my slow progress with a blend of pity. They saw me in the library, surrounded by piles of books, and assumed that my slow learning was a reflection of my abilities rather than the challenges I faced. Their pity felt like another form of rejection, a reminder that my efforts, though earnest, were not always understood.

The combination of these judgments and the disparity between my hard work and my results took a toll on me. I began to retreat into myself, the joy of learning overshadowed by the pressure of others' expectations and my own feelings of inadequacy.

As the weeks went by, I found myself sinking into a deeper sense of fatigue and depression. I would sit in my room, surrounded by textbooks that seemed more like a burden than a gateway to knowledge.

The once exciting campus had become a source of anxiety, filled with echoes of judgement.

I grappled with the harsh reality of my situation. My dreams of academic success seemed increasingly out of reach, clouded by growing despair. I questioned my path, wondering if I would ever be able to bridge the gap between my potential and my performance.

Chapter Nine

The Burden of Judgment

Amidst the struggles of university life, I found myself drawn to one of my male classmates. His focus and academic prowess were apparent, and I initially hoped that we could develop a close friendship.

As we began to interact more, it became clear that he had a sharp mind and a lot of confidence. However, it soon manifested into a cutting form of arrogance instead. His remarks, which started as casual observations, gradually turned into pointed criticisms.

He began to mock my struggles with concentration. He would make dismissive comments like, "You're so unfocused, you'd miss a meteor even if it were right in front of you."

His words stung more than he probably realised, and each jibe felt like a blow to my already fragile self-esteem.

During exams, his reactions were even more harsh. When he saw me make mistakes on what he considered easy questions,he would exclaim, "This question is so simple, how could you get it wrong? Even a child would know this answer!"

His anger was not only directed at the mistakes I made, but at my apparent inability to grasp what he saw as basic knowledge.

His criticism and mocking tone went beyond mere comments; it felt like a personal attack on my abilities. I would leave those interactions feeling even more deflated, questioning my competence and whether I would ever be able to meet the expectations of those around me.

I started to dread interactions with him, feeling increasingly scrutinised and self-conscious. I began to withdraw more, avoiding situations where I might be subjected to further criticism. The process of trying to build connections while dealing with such negativity became increasingly difficult.

Chapter Ten

Seeking Help

Feeling overwhelmed by the weight of my struggles, I made the decision to seek professional help. The thought of reaching out for support was both a relief and a source of anxiety. I scheduled an appointment with the university counsellor, hoping to find some guidance and relief from the despair that had been shadowing my days.

The day of the appointment arrived, and I walked into the counselling office with a mix of apprehension and hope. The office was a calm, inviting space, filled with soft lighting and comfortable chairs. The counsellor, a young woman with straight, short hair and a serene demeanour, greeted me with a warm smile. Her presence was reassuring, and I felt a glimmer of comfort in her calmness.

After we settled into our seats, she listened attentively as I spoke about my struggles with focus, academic pressure, and the emotional toll it had taken on me. I poured out my frustrations and fears, describing the harsh judgments from peers, the constant battle with distraction, and the growing sense of inadequacy that had begun to dominate my life.

When I finished, she took a moment to reflect on what I had shared. Her response was measured and compassionate.

"From what you've described, it seems like your feelings of depression and frustration might have deeper roots. It's clear that your current challenges are significant, but they could be part of a more underlying issue."

She suggested that my struggles might require more than just immediate support and recommended that I see an experienced psychotherapist for a more comprehensive evaluation.

After a moment of hesitation and weighing my options, I reluctantly agreed to follow her recommendation. The prospect of engaging in further therapy felt intimidating, yet I knew it was a step I needed to take. I wanted to understand and address the root causes of my difficulties, even if it meant

confronting aspects of my past and psyche
that I had avoided.

With a sense of cautious optimism, I
prepared for the next phase of my journey.
The path ahead was uncertain and
challenging, but I was determined to pursue
the help I needed.

Chapter Eleven

The First Step

I finally convinced myself to make an appointment with the psychotherapist. On a sunny afternoon, I set off for her office. As I sat on the bus, doubts crept into my mind. I wondered what my friends would think if they knew I was seeking help from a psychotherapist. The fear of judgement weighed heavy again, but I tried to push those thoughts aside, focusing on the hope that therapy might bring some relief.

The therapist's office was minimalist, with only a few tasteful decorations and a large window that let in natural light. She was a woman in her fifties with long hair tied neatly at the back of her head. She wore glasses and was dressed in a light blue outfit with matching accessories. Her warm attitude put me at ease as she welcomed me into her office.

She asked gently, "What brings you here today?"

"Depression," I replied, feeling a lump form in my throat.

She nodded empathetically and asked, "Can you describe the symptoms you're experiencing, or what made you feel like you're suffering from depression?"

I took a deep breath and started listing my symptoms, "I've been feeling very low, with little self-confidence. There's this overwhelming sense of hopelessness and lack of motivation. I constantly feel worthless and unable to control my problems or my life."

She listened intently, her eyes kind and understanding, "When did these symptoms start?"

I began to recount the various issues that had been piling up over time. I spoke about my struggles with focus and concentration, the harsh judgments from my peers, and the emotional toll it had taken on me. I described the feelings of inadequacy that seemed to shadow my every move and the constant battle against distractions that left me exhausted and disheartened.

As I spoke, she occasionally nodded, jotting down notes but always maintaining eye contact, making me feel heard and understood. I found myself opening up more than I had anticipated, revealing the depths of my frustration and sadness.

She gently probed further, asking about specific instances that had worsened my feelings of depression. I talked about my interactions with a male classmate who had initially seemed promising, but had turned out to be a source of harsh criticism and ridicule. His constant mockery and scornful remarks had chipped away at my already fragile self-esteem, leaving me feeling even more isolated and vulnerable.

The psychotherapist listened with unwavering attention, her compassionate presence offering a safe space for me to express my deepest fears and insecurities. As the session progressed, I felt a small sense of relief, as though a heavy burden was beginning to lift.

By the end of our conversation, She explained that our goal would be to explore the root causes of my depression and develop strategies to cope with my challenges more effectively. It was clear that this would be a journey, one that required patience and persistence.

As I left her office, I felt a mix of emotions—relief, apprehension, and a glimmer of hope.

Chapter Twelve

A New Perspective

I sat in the waiting room of the psychotherapist for my second session, my heart pounding against my ribcage. I fiddled with the strap of my bag, my eyes darting around the room. The walls were a soft shade of blue, designed to be calming, but it had little effect on me.

"Elizabeth, you can go in now," the receptionist called out, her voice pulling me out of my thoughts. I stood up, taking a deep breath, and walked into the office.

Dr. Collins greeted me with a warm smile, gesturing for me to take a seat. I sat down, feeling the weight of the silence in the room.

"It's good to see you again. How have you been?" Dr. Collins began.

"I've been okay, I guess. Just… a bit confused," I replied, my fingers still playing with the strap of my bag.

Dr. Collins nodded, her expression encouraging me to continue.

"I've been thinking a lot about what we talked about last time. You mentioned ADHD, and… I've heard the name, but I never thought I might be diagnosed with that. I think my problems are different," I said, my voice barely above a whisper.

Dr. Collins leaned forward slightly, her eyes focused on mine. "I understand. It's normal to feel that way. ADHD can be a complex and sometimes misunderstood condition.

What I'd like to do today is discuss my perspective on ADHD and its treatment, but I want to stress that this is my opinion. Other therapists might have different views because psychological issues aren't like organic or medical problems. There is a very broad spectrum."

My eyes widened slightly, curiosity piqued. Dr. Collins continued, her voice steady and reassuring.

"Unlike medical conditions, psychological issues like ADHD don't have a one-size-fits-all diagnosis or treatment. They vary greatly from person to person, and what works for one individual might not work for another. ADHD, in particular, is often seen as a disorder, but I believe it's more nuanced than that. In my opinion, ADHD isn't just a problem—it's different. It comes with both disadvantages and advantages."

I tilted my head, intrigued. "Advantages?" I asked, the word sounding foreign in this context.

Dr. Collins smiled, "Yes, advantages. There are several books that delve into this perspective, such as *The ADHD Advantage* by Dale Archer and another with the same title by Anders Hansen. These authors explain how the traits associated with ADHD can actually be strengths in certain areas."

I leaned forward, eager to hear more.

"People with ADHD often have high levels of creativity and can think outside the box. They are great at coming up with innovative solutions and can be incredibly resourceful. They also tend to be very passionate about their interests, which can drive them to achieve great things. Another advantage is their ability to hyperfocus. When they're interested in something, they can concentrate intensely for long periods, which can lead to high productivity and expertise in their chosen fields."

My mind raced as I processed this new information. The idea that my struggles could also be my strengths was liberating.

Dr. Collins leaned back, giving me a moment to absorb the information, "Of course, this doesn't mean that ADHD doesn't come with challenges. But understanding the full picture—seeing both the challenges and the potential advantages—can help you navigate your journey more effectively."

I nodded slowly, a small smile forming on my lips. Maybe my differences weren't just problems to be fixed, but unique traits that could be embraced and harnessed.

As the session continued, I found myself opening up more, sharing my experiences and fears. Dr. Collins listened intently, offering insights and practical advice. By the end of the hour, I felt lighter, as if a heavy burden had been lifted from my shoulders.

Chapter Thirteen

New Strategies

I left Dr. Collins's office with a mix of emotions swirling inside me. The sky was a soft grey, hinting at rain, and the cool breeze felt refreshing against my skin. I walked slowly, my mind replaying the session's conversation over and over.

Advantages of ADHD. The concept seemed foreign, almost like a paradox. Yet, as I considered it, fragments of my life began to fit into this new perspective. I made my way to a nearby café, deciding that a warm drink might help me process everything.

Sitting by the window with a steaming cup of coffee, I let my thoughts wander. I had always been creative, finding joy in painting and drawing since I was a child. My passion for art had been a constant in my life, a refuge during turbulent times. Maybe Dr. Collins was right—perhaps my ADHD was part of what fueled that creativity.

I pulled out my sketchbook, letting the pencil glide across the paper. My thoughts drifted to the idea of hyperfocus. I remembered the times I had lost myself in my artwork, hours passing by without my noticing. Those were the moments when I felt truly alive, completely immersed in my world.

But it wasn't just art. I recalled the school projects that had consumed me, the books I had devoured in a single sitting. When something captured my interest, I could dive in deeply, exploring every facet with an intensity that surprised even me.

I realised that this hyperfocus wasn't just a quirk—it was a strength. It allowed me to achieve a level of expertise and passion that others might not reach. I sipped my coffee, feeling a small spark of excitement.

Over the next few days, I continued to explore this new perspective. I read *The ADHD Advantage* by Dale Archer, captivated by the stories of people who had turned their ADHD into a strength. Each page resonated with me, echoing my experiences and offering new insights.

I also delved into Anders Hansen's book, finding it equally enlightening. The scientific explanations and real-life examples provided a solid foundation for understanding. These books painted a picture of ADHD not as a disorder, but as a different way of thinking and functioning—one that could be incredibly powerful.

In the evenings, I took long walks, allowing my mind to process everything. I found myself reflecting on my past, seeing patterns and connections that I hadn't noticed before. The struggles with attention, the restless energy, the bursts of creativity—all these traits were part of a larger mosaic.

I also began to notice the areas where ADHD had posed challenges. My disorganisation, the difficulty in managing time, the impulsivity—they were all part of the equation. But instead of viewing them as insurmountable obstacles, I started to see them as areas for growth.

I decided to implement some of the strategies suggested in the books. I started keeping a detailed planner, breaking down tasks into manageable steps. I created a dedicated space for my art, free from distractions, where I could let my creativity flow. I also set aside time for meditation and mindfulness, hoping to improve my focus and reduce anxiety.

As the days turned into weeks, I noticed subtle changes. I felt more in control, more balanced. My productivity increased, and I found myself enjoying my work more. There were still challenges, of course, but I faced them with a newfound confidence.

I also reached out to a few friends who had mentioned their struggles with ADHD in the past. We shared our experiences and strategies, offering support and encouragement to each other. It was comforting to know I wasn't alone, that others were navigating similar paths.

When it was time for my next appointment with Dr. Collins, I walked into her office with a sense of anticipation. I had so much to share, so many questions to ask. She greeted me with her usual warm smile, and I felt a wave of gratitude for her guidance.

"Elizabeth, it's good to see you. How have you been?" she asked, settling into her chair.

I took a deep breath, feeling the weight of the past few weeks lift off my shoulders.

"I've been… learning a lot," I said, a smile tugging at the corners of my mouth, "I've been reading, reflecting, and trying out new strategies. And it's been incredible. I'm starting to see everything in a new light."

Dr. Collins's eyes sparkled with interest, "That's wonderful to hear. Tell me more about what you've discovered."

As I shared my journey, the room seemed to brighten. Dr. Collins listened intently, offering insights and affirmations. We discussed the strategies that had worked for me and brainstormed ways to tackle the remaining challenges.

Chapter Fourteen

Embracing Change

Over the next few weeks, my sessions with Dr. Collins took on a new intensity. She introduced me to Cognitive Behavioral Therapy (CBT), a method she believed would help me manage my ADHD symptoms more effectively. From the outset, she made it clear that while she found this strategy useful, other therapists might prefer different approaches, and each person's journey with ADHD could require unique strategies.

"CBT focuses on identifying and changing negative thought patterns and behaviours," Dr. Collins explained during one of our sessions, "It's about understanding the connection between your thoughts, feelings, and actions. This approach can be particularly helpful for ADHD because it provides practical tools to manage daily challenges."

I nodded, eager to learn more. Dr. Collins handed me a book titled *Cognitive Behavioral Therapy for Adult ADHD* by J. Russell Ramsay. She suggested we use it as a guide for our sessions.

We began with identifying my negative thought patterns. Dr. Collins asked me to keep a journal, noting situations where I felt overwhelmed or discouraged. She told me to write down my thoughts and feelings in these moments, no matter how trivial they seemed.

During our next session, we reviewed my journal together. I noticed a pattern: I often felt inadequate and frustrated when tasks didn't go as planned. These feelings would spiral into self-doubt and procrastination, creating a vicious cycle.

"Let's challenge these thoughts," Dr. Collins said, "What evidence do you have that you're inadequate?"

I paused, thinking, "Well, I mess up a lot. I forget things, I'm late to classes, and I can't seem to stay organised."

"Those are behaviours, not evidence of inadequacy. What about the times when you've succeeded or done well?"

I reflected on her question. I remembered the science competition I had won in high school, the projects I had completed, and the times I had been a supportive friend. Slowly, I began to see that my negative thoughts weren't entirely accurate.

Dr. Collins introduced me to the concept of cognitive restructuring, "When you catch yourself thinking negatively, ask yourself if there's evidence to support that thought. If not, try to reframe it in a more balanced way."

We practised this together, using examples from my journal. When I thought, "I'm always late, I'm unreliable," Dr. Collins helped me reframe it: "I've been late before, but I'm working on improving my time management."

The next phase of CBT focused on behavioural strategies. Dr. Collins emphasised the importance of structure and routine. She suggested using a planner to organise my day, breaking tasks into smaller, manageable steps. We discussed prioritisation techniques, like the Eisenhower Matrix, to help me focus on what was truly important.

Dr. Collins also introduced mindfulness exercises to help me stay present and reduce anxiety. She recommended setting aside a few minutes each day for meditation, using apps like Headspace or Calm to guide me. These exercises aimed to improve my focus and help me manage stress.

Throughout our sessions, Dr. Collins frequently referred to *Rethinking Adult ADHD* by J. Russell Ramsay. The book provided additional insights into how CBT could be adapted for ADHD, emphasising the need for flexibility and creativity in treatment.

One particularly impactful session focused on procrastination. Dr. Collins explained that procrastination is often driven by fear of failure or perfectionism. We explored ways to break tasks into smaller steps and set realistic deadlines. She encouraged me to celebrate small victories, rather than waiting for perfect results.

As weeks turned into months, I noticed significant changes. My planner became an essential tool, helping me stay organised and on track. The mindfulness exercises brought a sense of calm and focus to my chaotic mind. Most importantly, I started to challenge my negative thoughts, replacing them with more balanced ones.

Dr. Collins's approach was compassionate yet firm. She pushed me to confront my fears and take responsibility for my progress. Each session left me feeling more empowered and capable.

One rainy afternoon, as I sat in her office, she smiled at me with a hint of pride, "Elizabeth, you've made remarkable progress. How do you feel about the journey so far?"

I took a moment to reflect, "I feel more in control. It's not that my ADHD is gone, but I'm learning to work with it, not against it."

Chapter Fifteen

Specific Tools

One day, Dr. Collins leaned forward, her eyes intent on mine, "Elizabeth, today I want to focus on some practical strategies that can help you manage common ADHD challenges, such as perfectionism and procrastination. One effective technique is the 'Just Do It' approach."

I tilted my head, curious, "Just Do It?"

"Yes," she nodded, "It's about taking immediate action without overthinking or waiting for the perfect moment. Perfectionism often paralyses us, making it hard to start tasks because we're afraid of not doing them perfectly. With 'Just Do It,' you commit to starting the task, no matter how imperfectly. The key is to engage with the work and build momentum."

I took a deep breath, thinking about all the times I had procrastinated because I feared my efforts wouldn't measure up.

"That makes sense. It's about breaking the cycle of inaction."

"Exactly. Another important aspect is avoiding what I call 'impulsive compliance.' This happens when you feel pressured to say yes to every request or demand, often because of a desire to please others or avoid conflict."

I nodded, recognizing myself in her words, "So, what should I do instead?"

"Practice saying, 'I need to think about your request.' This gives you time to evaluate whether you truly want to comply. Before responding, count to ten. This simple delay can help you make more thoughtful decisions."

I scribbled notes, appreciating the practicality of these suggestions.

Dr. Collins continued, "It's also important to address cognitive errors, which are common in ADHD. These include black-and-white thinking, overgeneralization, and catastrophizing. Let's discuss some of these in detail."

She explained each cognitive error with examples, helping me see how they distorted my thinking, "For instance, black-and-white thinking can make you see situations as all good or all bad, with no middle ground. Overgeneralization takes one negative event and applies it broadly, while catastrophizing exaggerates the importance of problems."

I sighed, realising how often I fell into these traps, "How do I counteract them?"

"One effective method is cognitive defusion. This technique helps you distance yourself from automatic thoughts. Instead of accepting them as truth, you observe them as mere thoughts. For example, if you think 'I'm a failure,' you can reframe it as 'I'm thinking that I'm a failure.' This subtle shift can reduce the power of negative thoughts."

"Another strategy," Dr. Collins added, "Is to make abstract goals concrete. ADHD often makes it difficult to pursue vague, long-term goals. By breaking them down into specific, tangible steps, you can track your progress and stay motivated."

We worked through one of my goals, turning it from a daunting aspiration into a series of actionable steps. The clarity this brought was immensely helpful.

"Finally," Dr. Collins said with a smile, "let's talk about the Premack Principle, also known as 'Grandma's Rule.' This principle suggests using preferred activities to reinforce less preferred ones. For instance, you might tell yourself, 'Once I finish this task, I can spend time painting',"

I grinned, liking the idea of rewarding myself with something I loved, "That sounds like a great motivator."

Dr. Collins nodded, "It's a powerful tool. And don't forget to celebrate your successes, no matter how small. Encouraging and rewarding yourself builds positive momentum and reinforces good habits."

As our sessions continued, I integrated these techniques into my daily life. When faced with a task, I reminded myself to 'Just Do It', diving in without waiting for the perfect conditions. I practised saying, "I need to think about your request," and counted to ten before making decisions. This pause helped me avoid impulsive commitments and gave me the space to consider my own needs.

I became more mindful of my cognitive errors, catching myself when I slipped into black-and-white thinking or catastrophizing. Cognitive defusion allowed me to detach from negative thoughts, reducing their impact on my mood and behaviour.

By breaking down abstract goals into concrete steps, I found a new sense of direction and purpose. Each small accomplishment was a victory, and I rewarded myself accordingly, using the Premack Principle to maintain motivation.

One evening, I sat at my desk, reflecting on my journey. My planner was filled with completed tasks, my sketchbook brimming with new ideas. The techniques Dr. Collins had taught me were transforming my life, helping me harness the potential of my ADHD rather than being overwhelmed by it.

Our sessions continued to be a source of support and growth. Dr. Collins's empathetic approach and practical advice made each visit a turning point. She encouraged me to keep exploring and adapting, reminding me that the journey was ongoing.

As I walked into her office for our next session, I felt a deep sense of gratitude.

Dr. Collins greeted me, "Elizabeth, How do you feel about your journey now?"

I took a moment to reflect, a smile spreading across my face, "I feel empowered. For the first time, I'm not just surviving with ADHD—I'm thriving."

Dr. Collins's eyes sparkled, "That's wonderful to hear. Remember, this is just one part of your journey. Keep exploring, keep learning, and most importantly, keep believing in yourself."

My journey with ADHD was far from over, but with the tools and support I had gained, I knew I was on the right path. Each day brought new challenges and opportunities, and I was ready to face them with confidence.

Chapter Sixteen

Navigating Relationships

In one of our sessions, I felt the need to delve deeper into my relationships. I had always found interactions with others challenging and often felt misunderstood. Dr. Collins listened attentively as I expressed my concerns.

"Why do I find it so hard to connect with people sometimes?"

She leaned forward, her expression thoughtful, "What you're experiencing is not uncommon for individuals with ADHD. While ADHD can affect social interactions, it's important to understand the underlying reasons. Some people with ADHD struggle with what we call 'social debt'."

"Social debt?" I echoed, intrigued.

"Yes," she nodded. "Social debt refers to the cumulative impact of repeated social misunderstandings and conflicts that have happened over time. For instance, impulsivity might lead you to interrupt others or say things without considering the consequences. Inattention might cause you to miss social cues or forget important details about someone's life. These behaviours can strain relationships and create a sense of social debt, where you feel like you're constantly making up for past mistakes."

I sighed, recognizing these patterns in my own life, "That makes sense. So, how do I manage this social debt?"

"First, it's crucial to become more aware of these tendencies. Practice active listening, and take a moment to think before you speak. Mindfulness exercises can help improve your attention in social settings. And remember, it's okay to apologise and explain your ADHD to others. Most people are understanding when they know where you're coming from."

I nodded, feeling a bit more hopeful. "What about romantic relationships? How do I explain my ADHD to a potential boyfriend?"

share your personality traits, including your ADHD. Explain how it affects you, both the strengths and the challenges. This helps set realistic expectations and understanding."

"But what if they don't understand me?" I asked, a hint of anxiety creeping into my voice.

"No one has the right to bully or demean you," Dr. Collins said firmly, "If someone reacts negatively or doesn't respect you, they're not the right person for you. A healthy relationship is built on mutual respect, empathy, and support. Make sure your partner understands that your ADHD is just one aspect of who you are and that it comes with unique strengths."

Her words gave me a sense of empowerment. I had often felt vulnerable in relationships, but now I understood the importance of setting boundaries and advocating for myself.

Our conversation then shifted to academics, another area where I struggled,

Dr. Collins smiled, "Honesty is key. When you start a relationship, it's important to "Studying has always been a challenge for me. I get bored easily and find it hard to stay focused."

She nodded, "That's a common issue for people with ADHD. The key is to make studying more engaging and enjoyable. One way to do this is by incorporating different sensory elements into your study routine."

I looked at her curiously, "What do you mean?"

"Try using colourful pens and notebooks for your notes. Visual stimulation can often make studying more interesting. You can also use highlighters to emphasise key points, create mind maps to visually organise information, or even incorporate movement by studying while standing or walking."

I felt a surge of excitement at the thought of making studying more interactive, "That sounds like it could actually be fun."

"Exactly," Dr. Collins agreed, "Another strategy is to break your study sessions into shorter, manageable chunks with regular breaks. This can help maintain your focus

and prevent burnout. Also, try to connect the material to your interests. For example, if you're studying history, think about how the events relate to art or other areas you're passionate about."

My interactions with others, my approach to relationships, and my study habits were all areas where I could apply these new strategies. Dr. Collins had provided me with tools that were practical, empowering, and tailored to my unique needs.

Over the following weeks, I put her advice into practice. I started using colourful pens and notebooks, creating visually appealing notes that made studying more engaging. I broke my study sessions into shorter intervals, giving myself time to recharge and stay focused. I also practised mindfulness and active listening in social situations, becoming more aware of my interactions and improving my connections with others.

When it came to relationships, I felt more confident in sharing my ADHD with potential partners. I realised that honesty and self-advocacy were crucial for building healthy, respectful relationships. I no longer felt the need to hide or apologise for it; instead, I embraced it as a part of who I was.

As the weeks turned into months, I noticed significant changes in my life. My relationships became more fulfilling, my academic performance improved, and my overall happiness increased.

Chapter Sixteen

Blossoming Potential

My journey continued with an unexpected turn: acceptance into a Pharmacy graduate program after my bachelor's degree. The acceptance letter felt like a validation of all the hard work, the struggles, and the relentless determination I had poured into my studies.

My ADHD, once a source of frustration, became an asset in many ways. I found myself thriving in the dynamic, demanding environment of the pharmacy program.

During my second year, I met Jacob. He was different from anyone I had ever known—patient, understanding, and deeply kind. Our paths crossed in a study group, and what began as a casual friendship quickly blossomed into something deeper. Jacob had a way of making me feel seen and appreciated for who I was, ADHD and all.

One evening, after a particularly gruelling exam week, Jacob and I were taking a walk through the university gardens. The air was crisp, and the leaves crunched beneath our feet. We talked about our dreams and aspirations, and I felt a connection that went beyond words.

"Elizabeth," he said, stopping to look at me, "I admire your resilience. You never let anything hold you back. I love that about you."

I smiled, feeling a warmth spread through me. As our relationship deepened, Jacob's unwavering support became a cornerstone of my life. He was there to celebrate my successes and offer comfort during the tough times. We were a perfect match, complementing each other's strengths and weaknesses.

Graduation day was a blur of excitement and joy. Standing on the stage, receiving my degree, I felt a profound sense of achievement. The journey had been long and challenging, but every moment had led to this triumphant point. Jacob was in the audience, cheering the loudest, his pride in me shining through.

Shortly after graduation, I was offered an excellent position at a prestigious pharmacy. It was a dream job, and I couldn't wait to dive into the work.

One evening, Jacob surprised me with a dinner date at our favourite restaurant. That night, he asked me to marry him, and I said yes.

As a pharmacist, I found ways to leverage the advantages of my ADHD every day. My creativity helped in developing patient care plans and improving workflow processes. I became known for my innovative approaches and my ability to handle high-pressure situations with ease.

Jacob and I built a life filled with love, laughter, and mutual support. He embraced my ADHD just as I had, understanding its quirks and celebrating its strengths. Together, we created a home where I could thrive, both personally and professionally.

As I stood there, I realised how far I had come. From a girl who struggled with inattentiveness and self-doubt to a successful pharmacist and a loving partner, my journey had been transformative. The tools and strategies I had learned from Dr. Collins, the support of my loved ones, and my own resilience had brought me to this moment.

One evening, as Jacob and I sat on our porch, watching the sunset, he turned to me with a smile, "Elizabeth, are you happy?"

I looked at him, my heart full, "Yes, I'm very happy. I've learned to embrace who I am, and I've found someone who loves me for all of it. What more could I ask for?"

As the sun dipped below the horizon, I felt a deep sense of peace. My ADHD was not a limitation; it was a unique part of my identity that brought strength, creativity, and resilience. With the right support and strategies, I knew I could achieve anything.

References

Archer, D. (2015). *The ADHD advantage: What you thought was a diagnosis may be your greatest strength*. Avery Publishing Group.

Hansen, A. (2021). *The ADHD advantage: How to turn your attention deficit disorder into a strength*. HarperCollins.

Ramsay, J. R. (2020). *Rethinking adult ADHD: Helping clients turn intentions into actions*. Guilford Press.

Images generated by:

- OpenAI's DALL·E

- Craiyon AI

- Gencraft AI

Milton Keynes UK
Ingram Content Group UK Ltd.
UKHW022011240924
448733UK00016B/914

9 798227 626844